The Hairy Ape

Eugene O'Neill

Contents

THE HAIRY APE

BY

Eugene O'Neill

"THE HAIRY APE"
A Comedy of Ancient and Modern Life

In Eight Scenes
By

EUGENE O'NEILL

CHARACTERS

ROBERT SMITH, "YANK"
PADDY
LONG
MILDRED DOUGLAS
HER AUNT
SECOND ENGINEER
A GUARD
A SECRETARY OF AN ORGANIZATION
STOKERS, LADIES, GENTLEMEN, ETC.

SCENE I

SCENE-- *The firemen's forecastle of a transatlantic liner an hour after sailing from New York for the voyage across. Tiers of narrow, steel bunks, three deep, on all sides. An entrance in rear. Benches on the floor before the bunks. The room is crowded with men, shouting, cursing, laughing, singing--a confused, inchoate uproar swelling into a sort of unity, a meaning--the bewildered, furious, baffled defiance of a beast in a cage. Nearly all the men are drunk. Many bottles are passed from hand to hand. All are dressed in dungaree pants, heavy ugly shoes. Some wear singlets, but the majority are stripped to the waist.*

The treatment of this scene, or of any other scene in the play, should by no means be naturalistic. The effect sought after is a cramped space in the bowels of a ship, imprisoned by white steel. The lines of bunks, the uprights supporting them, cross each other like the steel framework of a cage. The ceiling crushes down upon the men's heads. They cannot stand upright. This accentuates the natural stooping posture which shovelling coal and the resultant over-development of back and shoulder muscles have given them. The men themselves should resemble those pictures in which the appearance of Neanderthal Man is guessed at. All are hairy-chested, with long arms of tremendous power, and low, receding brows above their small, fierce, resentful eyes. All the civilized white races are represented, but except for the slight differentiation in color of hair, skin, eyes, all these men are alike.

The curtain rises on a tumult of sound. YANK is seated in the foreground. He seems broader, fiercer, more truculent, more powerful, more sure of himself than the rest. They respect his superior strength--the grudging respect of fear. Then, too, he represents to them a self-expression, the very last word in what they are, their most highly developed individual.

VOICES--Gif me trink dere, you!

'Ave a wet!

Salute!

Gesundheit!

Skoal!

Drunk as a lord, God stiffen you!

Here's how!

Luck!

Pass back that bottle, damn you!

Pourin' it down his neck!

Ho, Froggy! Where the devil have you been?

La Touraine.

I hit him smash in yaw, py Gott!

Jenkins--the First--he's a rotten swine--

And the coppers nabbed him--and I run--

I like peer better. It don't pig head gif you.

A slut, I'm sayin'! She robbed me aslape--

To hell with 'em all!

You're a bloody liar!

Say dot again!

[*Commotion. Two men about to fight are pulled apart.*]

No scrappin' now!

To-night--

See who's the best man!

Bloody Dutchman!

To-night on the for'ard square.

I'll bet on Dutchy.

He packa da wallop, I tella you!

Shut up, Wop!

No fightin', maties. We're all chums, ain't we?

[*A voice starts bawling a song.*]

"Beer, beer, glorious beer!
Fill yourselves right up to here."

YANK--[*For the first time seeming to take notice of the uproar about him, turns around threateningly--in a tone of contemptuous authority.*] "Choke off dat noise! Where d'yuh get dat beer stuff? Beer, hell! Beer's for goils--and Dutchmen. Me for somep'n wit a kick to it! Gimme a drink, one of youse guys. [*Several bottles are eagerly offered. He takes a tremendous gulp at one of them; then, keeping the bottle in his hand, glares belligerently at the owner, who hastens to acquiesce in this robbery by saying:*] All righto, Yank. Keep it and have another." [*Yank contemptuously turns his back on the crowd again. For a second there is an embarrassed silence. Then--*]

VOICES--We must be passing the Hook. She's beginning to roll to it. Six days in hell--and then Southampton. Py Yesus, I vish somepody take my first vatch for me! Gittin' seasick, Square-head? Drink up and forget it! What's in your bottle? Gin. Dot's nigger trink. Absinthe? It's doped. You'll go off your chump, Froggy! Cochon! Whiskey, that's the ticket! Where's Paddy? Going asleep. Sing us that whiskey song, Paddy. [*They all turn to an old, wizened Irishman who is dozing, very drunk, on the benches forward. His face is extremely monkey-like with all the sad, patient pathos of that animal in his small eyes.*] Singa da song, Caruso Pat! He's gettin' old. The drink is too much for him. He's too drunk.

PADDY--[*Blinking about him, starts to his feet resentfully, swaying, holding on to the edge of a bunk.*] I'm never too drunk to sing. 'Tis only when I'm dead to the world I'd be wishful to sing at all. [***With a sort of sad contempt.***] "Whiskey Johnny," ye want? A chanty, ye want? Now that's a queer wish from the ugly like of you, God help you. But no matther. [***He starts to sing in a thin, nasal, doleful tone:***]

Oh, whiskey is the life of man!
Whiskey! O Johnny!

[***They all join in on this.***]

Oh, whiskey is the life of man!
Whiskey for my Johnny! [***Again chorus***]
Oh, whiskey drove my old man mad!
Whiskey! O Johnny!
Oh, whiskey drove my old man mad!
Whiskey for my Johnny!

YANK--[***Again turning around scornfully.***] Aw hell! Nix on dat old sailing ship stuff! All dat bull's dead, see? And you're dead, too, yuh damned old Harp, on'y yuh don't know it. Take it easy, see. Give us a rest. Nix on de loud noise. [***With a cynical grin.***] Can't youse see I'm tryin' to t'ink?

ALL--[***Repeating the word after him as one with same cynical amused mockery.***] Think! [***The chorused word has a brazen metallic quality as if their throats were phonograph horns. It is followed by a general uproar of hard, barking laughter.***]

VOICES--Don't be cracking your head wid ut, Yank.

You gat headache, py yingo!

One thing about it--it rhymes with drink!

Ha, ha, ha!

Drink, don't think!

Drink, don't think!

Drink, don't think!

[*A whole chorus of voices has taken up this refrain, stamping on the floor, pounding on the benches with fists.*]

YANK--[*Taking a gulp from his bottle--good-naturedly.*] Aw right. Can de noise. I got yuh de foist time. [*The uproar subsides. A very drunken sentimental tenor begins to sing:*]

"Far away in Canada,
Far across the sea,
There's a lass who fondly waits
Making a home for me--"

YANK--[*Fiercely contemptuous.*] Shut up, yuh lousey boob! Where d'yuh get dat tripe? Home? Home, hell! I'll make a home for yuh! I'll knock yuh dead. Home! T'hell wit home! Where d'yuh get dat tripe? Dis is home, see? What d'yuh want wit home? [*Proudly.*] I runned away from mine when I was a kid. On'y too glad to beat it, dat was me. Home was lickings for me, dat's all. But yuh can bet your shoit noone ain't never licked me since! Wanter try it, any of youse? Huh! I guess not. [*In a more placated but still contemptuous tone.*] Goils waitin' for yuh, huh? Aw, hell! Dat's all tripe. Dey don't wait for noone. Dey'd double-cross yuh for a nickel. Dey're all tarts, get me? Treat 'em rough, dat's me. To hell wit 'em. Tarts, dat's what, de whole bunch of 'em.

LONG--[*Very drunk, jumps on a bench excitedly, gesticulating with a bottle in his hand.*] Listen 'ere, Comrades! Yank 'ere is right. 'E says this 'ere stinkin' ship is our 'ome. And 'e says as 'ome is 'ell. And 'e's right! This is 'ell. We lives in 'ell, Comrades--and right enough we'll die in it. [*Raging.*] And who's ter blame, I arsks yer? We ain't. We wasn't born this rotten way. All men is born free and ekal. That's in the bleedin' Bible, maties. But what d'they care for the Bible--them lazy, bloated swine what travels first cabin? Them's the ones. They dragged us down 'til we're on'y wage slaves in the bowels of a bloody ship, sweatin', burnin' up, eatin' coal dust! Hit's them's ter blame--the damned capitalist clarss! [*There had been a gradual murmur of contemptuous resentment rising among the men until now he is interrupted by a storm of catcalls, hisses, boos, hard laughter.*]

VOICES--Turn it off!

Shut up!

Sit down!

Closa da face!

Tamn fool! (Etc.)

YANK--[*Standing up and glaring at Long.*] Sit down before I knock yuh down! [*Long makes haste to efface himself. Yank goes on contemptuously.*] De Bible, huh? De Cap'tlist class, huh? Aw nix on dat Salvation Army-Socialist bull. Git a soapbox! Hire a hall! Come and be saved, huh? Jerk us to Jesus, huh? Aw g'wan! I've listened to lots of guys like you, see, Yuh're all wrong. Wanter know what I t'ink? Yuh ain't no good for noone. Yuh're de bunk. Yuh ain't got no noive, get me? Yuh're yellow, dat's what. Yellow, dat's you. Say! What's dem slobs in de foist cabin got to do wit us? We're better men dan dey are, ain't we? Sure! One of us guys could clean up de whole mob wit one mit. Put one of 'em down here for one watch in de stokehole, what'd happen? Dey'd carry him off on a stretcher. Dem boids don't amount to nothin'. Dey're just baggage. Who makes dis old tub run? Ain't it us guys? Well den, we belong, don't we? We belong and dey don't. Dat's all. [*A loud chorus of approval. Yank goes on*] As for dis bein' hell--aw, nuts! Yuh lost your noive, dat's what. Dis is a man's job, get me? It belongs. It runs dis tub. No stiffs need apply. But yuh're a stiff, see? Yuh're yellow, dat's you.

VOICES--[*With a great hard pride in them.*]

Righto!

A man's job!

Talk is cheap, Long.

He never could hold up his end.

Divil take him!

Yank's right. We make it go.

Py Gott, Yank say right ting!

We don't need noone cryin' over us.

Makin' speeches.

Throw him out!

Yellow!

Chuck him overboard!

I'll break his jaw for him!

[*They crowd around Long threateningly.*]

YANK--[*Half good-natured again--contemptuously.*] Aw, take it easy. Leave him alone. He ain't woith a punch. Drink up. Here's how, whoever owns dis. [*He takes a long swallow from his bottle. All drink with him. In a flash all is hilarious amiability again, back-slapping, loud talk, etc.*]

PADDY--[*Who has been sitting in a blinking, melancholy daze--suddenly cries out in a voice full of old sorrow.*] We belong to this, you're saying? We make the ship to go, you're saying? Yerra then, that Almighty God have pity on us! [*His voice runs into the wail of a keen, he rocks back and forth on his bench. The men stare at him, startled and impressed in spite of themselves.*] Oh, to be back in the fine days of my youth, ochone! Oh, there was fine beautiful ships them days--clippers wid tall masts touching the sky--fine strong men in them--men that was sons of the sea as if 'twas the mother that bore them. Oh, the clean skins of them, and the clear eyes, the straight backs and full chests of them! Brave men they was, and bold men surely! We'd be sailing out, bound down round the Horn maybe. We'd be making sail in the dawn, with a fair breeze, singing a chanty song wid no care to it. And astern the land would be sinking low and dying out, but we'd give it no heed but a laugh, and never a look behind. For the day that was, was enough, for we was free men--and I'm thinking 'tis only slaves do be giving heed to the day that's gone or the day to come--until they're old like me. [*With a sort of religious exaltation.*] Oh, to be scudding south again wid the power of the Trade Wind driving her on steady through the nights and the days! Full sail on her! Nights and days! Nights when the foam of the wake would be flaming wid fire, when the sky'd be blazing and winking wid stars. Or the full of the moon maybe. Then you'd see her driving through the gray night, her sails stretching aloft all silver and white, not a sound on the deck, the lot of us dreaming dreams, till you'd believe 'twas no real ship at all you was on but a ghost ship like the Flying Dutchman they say does be roaming the seas forevermore widout touching a port. And there was the days, too. A warm sun on the clean decks. Sun warming the blood of you, and wind over the miles of shiny green ocean like strong drink to your lungs. Work--aye, hard work--but who'd mind that at all? Sure, you worked under the sky and 'twas work wid skill and daring to it. And wid the day done, in the dog watch, smoking me pipe at ease, the lookout would be raising land maybe, and we'd see the mountains of South Americy wid the red fire of the setting sun painting their white tops and the clouds floating by them! [*His tone of exaltation ceases. He goes on mournfully.*] Yerra, what's the use of talking? 'Tis a dead man's whisper. [*To Yank resentfully.*] 'Twas them days men belonged to ships, not now. 'Twas them days a ship was part of the sea, and a man was part of a ship, and the sea joined all together and made it one. [*Scornfully.*] Is it one wid this you'd be, Yank--black smoke from the funnels smudging the sea, smudging the decks--the bloody engines pounding and throbbing and shaking--wid divil a sight of sun or a breath of clean air--choking our lungs wid coal dust--breaking our backs and hearts in the hell of the stokehole--feeding the bloody furnace--feeding our lives along wid the coal, I'm thinking--caged in by steel from a sight of the sky like bloody apes in the Zoo! [*With a harsh laugh.*] Ho-ho, divil mend you! Is it to belong to that you're wishing? Is it a flesh and blood wheel of the engines you'd be?

YANK--[***Who has been listening with a contemptuous sneer, barks out the answer.***] Sure ting! Dat's me! What about it?

PADDY--[***As if to himself--with great sorrow.***] Me time is past due. That a great wave wid sun in the heart of it may sweep me over the side sometime I'd be dreaming of the days that's gone!

YANK--Aw, yuh crazy Mick! [***He springs to his feet and advances on Paddy threateningly--then stops, fighting some queer struggle within himself--lets his hands fall to his sides--contemptuously.***] Aw, take it easy. Yuh're aw right, at dat. Yuh're bugs, dat's all--nutty as a cuckoo. All dat tripe yuh been pullin'--Aw, dat's all right. On'y it's dead, get me? Yuh don't belong no more, see. Yuh don't get de stuff. Yuh're too old. [***Disgustedly.***] But aw say, come up for air onct in a while, can't yuh? See what's happened since yuh croaked. [***He suddenly bursts forth vehemently, growing more and more excited.***] Say! Sure! Sure I meant it! What de hell--Say, lemme talk! Hey! Hey, you old Harp! Hey, youse guys! Say, listen to me--wait a moment--I gotter talk, see. I belong and he don't. He's dead but I'm livin'. Listen to me! Sure I'm part of de engines! Why de hell not! Dey move, don't dey? Dey're speed, ain't dey? Dey smash trou, don't dey? Twenty-five knots a hour! Dat's goin' some! Dat's new stuff! Dat belongs! But him, he's too old. He gets dizzy. Say, listen. All dat crazy tripe about nights and days; all dat crazy tripe about stars and moons; all dat crazy tripe about suns and winds, fresh air and de rest of it--Aw hell, dat's all a dope dream! Hittin' de pipe of de past, dat's what he's doin'. He's old and don't belong no more. But me, I'm young! I'm in de pink! I move wit it! It, get me! I mean de ting dat's de guts of all dis. It ploughs trou all de tripe he's been sayin'. It blows dat up! It knocks dat dead! It slams dat off en de face of de oith! It, get me! De engines and de coal and de smoke and all de rest of it! He can't breathe and swallow coal dust, but I kin, see? Dat's fresh air for me! Dat's food for me! I'm new, get me? Hell in de stokehole? Sure! It takes a man to work in hell. Hell, sure, dat's my fav'rite climate. I eat it up! I git fat on it! It's me makes it hot! It's me makes it roar! It's me makes it move! Sure, on'y for me everyting stops. It all goes dead, get me? De noise and smoke and all de engines movin' de woild, dey stop. Dere ain't nothin' no more! Dat's what I'm sayin'. Everyting else dat makes de woild move, somep'n makes it move. It can't move witout somep'n else, see? Den yuh get down to me. I'm at de bottom, get me! Dere ain't nothin' foither. I'm de end! I'm de start! I start somep'n and de woild moves! It--dat's me!--de new dat's moiderin' de old! I'm de ting in coal dat makes it boin; I'm steam and oil for de engines; I'm de ting in noise dat makes yuh hear it; I'm smoke and express trains and steamers and factory whistles; I'm de ting in gold dat makes it money! And I'm what makes iron into steel! Steel, dat stands for de whole ting! And I'm steel--steel--steel! I'm de muscles in steel, de punch behind it! [*As he says this he pounds with his fist against the steel bunks. All the men, roused to a pitch of frenzied self-glorification by his speech, do likewise. There is a deafening metallic roar, through which Yank's voice can be heard bellowing.*] Slaves, hell! We run de whole woiks. All de rich guys dat tink dey're somep'n, dey ain't nothin'! Dey don't belong. But us guys, we're in de move, we're at de bottom, de whole ting is us! [*Paddy from the start of Yank's speech has been taking one gulp after another from his bottle, at first frightenedly, as if he were afraid to listen, then desperately, as if to drown his senses, but finally has achieved complete indifferent, even amused, drunkenness. Yank sees his lips moving. He quells the uproar with a shout.*] Hey, youse guys, take it easy! Wait a moment! De nutty Harp is sayin' someth'n.

PADDY--[*Is heard now--throws his head back with a mocking burst of laughter.*] Ho-ho-ho-ho-ho---

YANK--[***Drawing back his fist, with a snarl.***] Aw! Look out who yuh're givin' the bark!

PADDY--[***Begins to sing the "Muler of Dee" with enormous good-nature.***]

"I care for nobody, no, not I,
And nobody cares for me."

YANK--[***Good-natured himself in a flash, interrupts PADDY with a slap on the bare back like a report.***] Dat's de stuff! Now yuh're gettin' wise to somep'n. Care for nobody, dat's de dope! To hell wit 'em all! And nix on nobody else carin'. I kin care for myself, get me! [***Eight bells sound, muffled, vibrating through the steel walls as if some enormous brazen gong were imbedded in the heart of the ship. All the men jump up mechanically, fie through the door silently close upon each other's heels in what is very like a prisoners lockstep. YANK slaps PADDY on the back.***] Our watch, yuh old Harp! [***Mockingly.***] Come on down in hell. Eat up de coal dust. Drink in de heat. It's it, see! Act like yuh liked it, yuh better--or croak yuhself.

PADDY--[***With jovial defiance.***] To the divil wid it! I'll not report this watch. Let thim log me and be damned. I'm no slave the like of you. I'll be sittin' here at me ease, and drinking, and thinking, and dreaming dreams.

YANK--[***Contemptuously.***] Tinkin' and dreamin', what'll that get yuh? What's tinkin' got to do wit it? We move, don't we? Speed, ain't it? Fog, dat's all you stand for. But we drive trou dat, don't we? We split dat up and smash trou--twenty-five knots a hour! [***Turns his back on Paddy scornfully.***] Aw, yuh make me sick! Yuh don't belong! [***He strides out the door in rear. Paddy hums to himself, blinking drowsily.***]

[*Curtain*]

SCENE II

SCENE--Two days out. A section of the promenade deck. MILDRED DOUG-LAS
and her aunt are discovered reclining in deck chairs. The former is a
girl of twenty, slender, delicate, with a pale, pretty face marred by a
self-conscious expression of disdainful superiority. She looks fretful,
nervous and discontented, bored by her own anemia. Her aunt is a
pompous and proud--and fat--old lady. She is a type even to the point
of a double chin and lorgnettes. She is dressed pretentiously, as if
afraid her face alone would never indicate her position in life.
MILDRED is dressed all in white.

The impression to be conveyed by this scene is one of the beautiful,
vivid life of the sea all about--sunshine on the deck in a great flood,
the fresh sea wind blowing across it. In the midst of this, these two
incongruous, artificial figures, inert and disharmonious, the elder
like a gray lump of dough touched up with rouge, the younger looking as
if the vitality of her stock had been sapped before she was conceived,
so that she is the expression not of its life energy but merely of the
artificialities that energy had won for itself in the spending.

MILDRED--[*Looking up with affected dreaminess.*] How the black smoke
swirls back against the sky! Is it not beautiful?

AUNT--[*Without looking up.*] I dislike smoke of any kind.

MILDRED--My great-grandmother smoked a pipe--a clay pipe.

AUNT--[*Ruffling.*] Vulgar!

MILDRED--She was too distant a relative to be vulgar. Time mellows pipes.

AUNT--[*Pretending boredom but irritated.*] Did the sociology you took up at college teach you that--to play the ghoul on every possible occasion, excavating old bones? Why not let your great-grandmother rest in her grave?

MILDRED--[*Dreamily.*] With her pipe beside her--puffing in Paradise.

AUNT--[*With spite.*] Yes, you are a natural born ghoul. You are even getting to look like one, my dear.

MILDRED--[*In a passionless tone.*] I detest you, Aunt. [*Looking at her critically.*] Do you know what you remind me of? Of a cold pork pudding against a background of linoleum tablecloth in the kitchen of a--but the possibilities are wearisome. [*She closes her eyes.*]

AUNT--[*With a bitter laugh.*] Merci for your candor. But since I am and must be your chaperone--in appearance, at least--let us patch up some sort of armed truce. For my part you are quite free to indulge any pose of eccentricity that beguiles you--as long as you observe the amenities--

MILDRED--[*Drawling.*] The inanities?

AUNT--[*Going on as if she hadn't heard.*] After exhausting the morbid thrills of social service work on New York's East Side--how they must have hated you, by the way, the poor that you made so much poorer in their own eyes!--you are now bent on making your slumming international. Well, I hope Whitechapel will provide the needed nerve tonic. Do not ask me to chaperone you there, however. I told your father I would not. I loathe deformity. We will hire an army of detectives and you may investigate everything--they allow you to see.

MILDRED--[*Protesting with a trace of genuine earnestness.*] Please do not mock at my attempts to discover how the other half lives. Give me credit for some sort of groping sincerity in that at least. I would like to help them. I would like to be some use in the world. Is it my fault I don't know how? I would like to be sincere, to touch life somewhere. [*With weary bitterness.*] But I'm afraid I have neither the vitality nor integrity. All that was burnt out in our stock before I was born. Grandfather's blast furnaces, flaming to the sky, melting steel, making millions--then father keeping those home fires burning, making more millions--and little me at the tail-end of it all. I'm a waste product in the Bessemer process--like the millions. Or rather, I inherit the acquired trait of the by-product, wealth, but none of the energy, none of the strength of the steel that made it. I am sired by gold and darned by it, as they say at the race track--damned in more ways than one, [*She laughs mirthlessly*].

AUNT--[*Unimpressed--superciliously.*] You seem to be going in for sincerity to-day. It isn't becoming to you, really--except as an obvious pose. Be as artificial as you are, I advise. There's a sort of sincerity in that, you know. And, after all, you must confess you like that better.

MILDRED--[*Again affected and bored.*] Yes, I suppose I do. Pardon me for my outburst. When a leopard complains of its spots, it must sound rather grotesque. [*In a mocking tone.*] Purr, little leopard. Purr, scratch, tear, kill, gorge yourself and be happy--only stay in the jungle where your spots are camouflage. In a cage they make you conspicuous.

AUNT--I don't know what you are talking about.

MILDRED--It would be rude to talk about anything to you. Let's just talk. [*She looks at her wrist watch.*] Well, thank goodness, it's about time for them to come for me. That ought to give me a new thrill, Aunt.

AUNT--[*Affectedly troubled.*] You don't mean to say you're really going? The dirt--the heat must be frightful--

MILDRED--Grandfather started as a puddler. I should have inherited an immunity to heat that would make a salamander shiver. It will be fun to put it to the test.

AUNT--But don't you have to have the captain's--or someone's--permission to visit the stokehole?

MILDRED--[*With a triumphant smile.*] I have it--both his and the chief engineer's. Oh, they didn't want to at first, in spite of my social service credentials. They didn't seem a bit anxious that I should investigate how the other half lives and works on a ship. So I had to tell them that my father, the president of Nazareth Steel, chairman of the board of directors of this line, had told me it would be all right.

AUNT--He didn't.

MILDRED--How naive age makes one! But I said he did, Aunt. I even said he had given me a letter to them--which I had lost. And they were afraid to take the chance that I might be lying. [*Excitedly.*] So it's

ho! for the stokehole. The second engineer is to escort me. [*Looking at her watch again.*] It's time. And here he comes, I think. [*The SECOND ENGINEER enters, He is a husky, fine-looking man of thirty-five*
or so. He stops before the two and tips his cap, visibly embarrassed and ill-at-ease.]

SECOND ENGINEER--Miss Douglas?

MILDRED--Yes. [*Throwing off her rugs and getting to her feet.*] Are we all ready to start?

SECOND ENGINEER--In just a second, ma'am. I'm waiting for the Fourth. He's coming along.

MILDRED--[*With a scornful smile.*] You don't care to shoulder this responsibility alone, is that it?

SECOND ENGINEER--[*Forcing a smile.*] Two are better than one. [*Disturbed by her eyes, glances out to sea--blurts out.*] A fine day we're having.

MILDRED--Is it?

SECOND ENGINEER--A nice warm breeze--

MILDRED--It feels cold to me.

SECOND ENGINEER--But it's hot enough in the sun--

MILDRED--Not hot enough for me. I don't like Nature. I was never athletic.

SECOND ENGINEER--[*Forcing a smile.*] Well, you'll find it hot enough where you're going.

MILDRED--Do you mean hell?

SECOND ENGINEER--[*Flabbergasted, decides to laugh.*] Ho-ho! No, I mean the stokehole.

MILDRED--My grandfather was a puddler. He played with boiling steel.

SECOND ENGINEER--[*All at sea--uneasily.*] Is that so? Hum, you'll excuse me, ma'am, but are you intending to wear that dress.

MILDRED--Why not?

SECOND ENGINEER--You'll likely rub against oil and dirt. It can't be helped.

MILDRED--It doesn't matter. I have lots of white dresses.

SECOND ENGINEER--I have an old coat you might throw over--

MILDRED--I have fifty dresses like this. I will throw this one into the sea when I come back. That ought to wash it clean, don't you think?

SECOND ENGINEER--[*Doggedly.*] There's ladders to climb down that are none too clean--and dark alleyways--

MILDRED--I will wear this very dress and none other.

SECOND ENGINEER--No offence meant. It's none of my business. I was only warning you--

MILDRED--Warning? That sounds thrilling.

SECOND ENGINEER--[*Looking down the deck--with a sigh of relief.*]--There's the Fourth now. He's waiting for us. If you'll come--

MILDRED--Go on. I'll follow you. [*He goes. Mildred turns a mocking smile on her aunt.*] An oaf--but a handsome, virile oaf.

AUNT--[*Scornfully.*] Poser!

MILDRED--Take care. He said there were dark alleyways--

AUNT--[*In the same tone.*] Poser!

MILDRED--[*Biting her lips angrily.*] You are right. But would that my millions were not so anemically chaste!

AUNT--Yes, for a fresh pose I have no doubt you would drag the name of Douglas in the gutter!

MILDRED--From which it sprang. Good-by, Aunt. Don't pray too hard that I may fall into the fiery furnace.

AUNT--Poser!

MILDRED--[*Viciously.*] Old hag! [*She slaps her aunt insultingly across the face and walks off, laughing gaily.*]

AUNT--[*Screams after her.*] I said poser!

[*Curtain*]

SCENE III

SCENE--The stokehole. In the rear, the dimly-outlined bulks of the
furnaces and boilers. High overhead one hanging electric bulb sheds
just enough light through the murky air laden with coal dust to pile up
masses of shadows everywhere. A line of men, stripped to the waist, is
before the furnace doors. They bend over, looking neither to right nor
left, handling their shovels as if they were part of their bodies, with
a strange, awkward, swinging rhythm. They use the shovels to throw open
the furnace doors. Then from these fiery round holes in the black a
flood of terrific light and heat pours full upon the men who are
outlined in silhouette in the crouching, inhuman attitudes of chained
gorillas. The men shovel with a rhythmic motion, swinging as on a pivot
from the coal which lies in heaps on the floor behind to hurl it into
the flaming mouths before them. There is a tumult of noise--the brazen
clang of the furnace doors as they are flung open or slammed shut, the
grating, teeth-gritting grind of steel against steel, of crunching
coal. This clash of sounds stuns one's ears with its rending
dissonance. But there is order in it, rhythm, a mechanical regulated
recurrence, a tempo. And rising above all, making the air hum with the
quiver of liberated energy, the roar of leaping flames in the furnaces,
the monotonous throbbing beat of the engines.

As the curtain rises, the furnace doors are shut. The men are taking a
breathing spell. One or two are arranging the coal behind them, pulling
it into more accessible heaps. The others can be dimly made out leaning
on their shovels in relaxed attitudes of exhaustion.

PADDY--[***From somewhere in the line--plaintively.***] Yerra, will this divil's own watch nivir end? Me back is broke. I'm destroyed entirely.

YANK--[*From the center of the line--with exuberant scorn.*] Aw, yuh make me sick! Lie down and croak, why don't yuh? Always beefin', dat's you! Say, dis is a cinch! Dis was made for me! It's my meat, get me! [*A whistle is blown--a thin, shrill note from somewhere overhead in the darkness. Yank curses without resentment.*] Dere's de damn engineer crakin' de whip. He tinks we're loafin'.

PADDY--[*Vindictively.*] God stiffen him!

YANK--[*In an exultant tone of command.*] Come on, youse guys! Git into de game! She's gittin' hungry! Pile some grub in her! Trow it into her belly! Come on now, all of youse! Open her up! [*At this last all the men, who have followed his movements of getting into position, throw open their furnace doors with a deafening clang. The fiery light floods over their shoulders as they bend round for the coal. Rivulets of sooty sweat have traced maps on their backs. The enlarged muscles form bunches of high light and shadow.*]

YANK--[*Chanting a count as he shovels without seeming effort.*] One--two--tree--[*His voice rising exultantly in the joy of battle.*] Dat's de stuff! Let her have it! All togedder now! Sling it into her! Let her ride! Shoot de piece now! Call de toin on her! Drive her into it! Feel her move! Watch her smoke! Speed, dat's her middle name! Give her coal, youse guys! Coal, dat's her booze! Drink it up, baby! Let's see yuh sprint! Dig in and gain a lap! Dere she go-o-es [*This last in the chanting formula of the gallery gods at the six-day bike race. He slams his furnace door shut. The others do likewise with as much unison as their wearied bodies will permit. The effect is of one fiery eye after another being blotted out with a series of accompanying bangs.*]

PADDY--[*Groaning.*] Me back is broke. I'm bate out--bate--[*There is a pause. Then the inexorable whistle sounds again from the dim regions above the electric light. There is a growl of cursing rage from all sides.*]

YANK--[*Shaking his fist upward--contemptuously.*] Take it easy dere, you! Who d'yuh tinks runnin' dis game, me or you? When I git ready, we move. Not before! When I git ready, get me!

VOICES--[*Approvingly.*] That's the stuff!

Yank tal him, py golly!

Yank ain't affeerd.

Goot poy, Yank!

Give him hell!

Tell 'im 'e's a bloody swine!

Bloody slave-driver!

YANK--[*Contemptuously.*] He ain't got no noive. He's yellow, get me? All de engineers is yellow. Dey got streaks a mile wide. Aw, to hell wit him! Let's move, youse guys. We had a rest. Come on, she needs it! Give her pep! It ain't for him. Him and his whistle, dey don't belong. But we belong, see! We gotter feed de baby! Come on! [*He turns and flings his furnace door open. They all follow his lead. At this instant the Second and Fourth Engineers enter from the darkness on the left with Mildred between them. She starts, turns paler, her pose is crumbling, she shivers with fright in spite of the blazing heat, but forces herself to leave the Engineers and take a few steps nearer the men. She is right behind Yank. All this happens quickly while the men have their backs turned.*]

YANK--Come on, youse guys! [*He is turning to get coal when the whistle sounds again in a peremptory, irritating note. This drives Yank into a sudden fury. While the other men have turned full around and stopped dumfounded by the spectacle of Mildred standing there in her white dress, Yank does not turn far enough to see her. Besides, his head is thrown back, he blinks upward through the murk trying to find the owner of the whistle, he brandishes his shovel murderously over his head in one hand, pounding on his chest, gorilla-like, with the other, shouting:*] Toin off dat whistle! Come down outa dere, yuh yellow, brass-buttoned, Belfast bum, yuh! Come down and I'll knock yer brains out! Yuh lousey, stinkin', yellow mut of a Catholic-moiderin' bastard! Come down and I'll moider yuh! Pullin' dat whistle on me, huh? I'll show yuh! I'll crash yer skull in! I'll drive yer teet' down yer troat! I'll slam yer nose trou de back of yer head! I'll cut yer guts out for a nickel, yuh lousey boob, yuh dirty, crummy, muck-eatin' son of a--

[*Suddenly he becomes conscious of all the other men staring at something directly behind his back. He whirls defensively with a snarling, murderous growl, crouching to spring, his lips drawn back o'ver his teeth, his small eyes gleaming ferociously. He sees Mildred, like a white apparition in the full light from the open furnace doors. He glares into her eyes, turned to stone. As for her, during his speech she has listened, paralyzed with horror, terror, her whole personality crushed, beaten in, collapsed, by the terrific impact of this unknown, abysmal brutality, naked and shameless. As she looks at his gorilla face, as his eyes bore into hers, she utters a low, choking cry and shrinks away from him, putting both hands up before her eyes to shut*

*out the sight of his face, to protect her own. This startles Yank to a
reaction. His mouth falls open, his eyes grow bewildered.*]

MILDRED--[*About to faint--to the Engineers, who now have her one by
each arm--whimperingly.*] Take me away! Oh, the filthy beast! [*She
faints. They carry her quickly back, disappearing in the darkness at
the left, rear. An iron door clangs shut. Rage and bewildered fury rush
back on Yank. He feels himself insulted in some unknown fashion in the
very heart of his pride. He roars:*] God damn yuh! [*And hurls his
shovel after them at the door which has just closed. It hits the steel
bulkhead with a clang and falls clattering on the steel floor. From
overhead the whistle sounds again in a long, angry, insistent command.*]

[*Curtain*]

SCENE IV

SCENE--The firemen's forecastle. Yank's watch has just come off duty
and had dinner. Their faces and bodies shine from a soap and water
scrubbing but around their eyes, where a hasty dousing does not touch,
the coal dust sticks like black make-up, giving them a queer, sinister
expression. Yank has not washed either face or body. He stands out in
contrast to them, a blackened, brooding figure. He is seated forward on
a bench in the exact attitude of Rodin's "The Thinker." The others,
most of them smoking pipes, are staring at Yank half-apprehensively, as
if fearing an outburst; half-amusedly, as if they saw a joke somewhere
that tickled them.

VOICES--He ain't ate nothin'.

Py golly, a fallar gat gat grub in him.

Divil a lie.

Yank feeda da fire, no feeda da face.

Ha-ha.

He ain't even washed hisself.

He's forgot.

Hey, Yank, you forgot to wash.

YANK--[*Sullenly.*] Forgot nothin'! To hell wit washin'.

VOICES--It'll stick to you. It'll get under your skin. Give yer the bleedin' itch, that's wot. It makes spots on you--like a leopard. Like a piebald nigger, you mean. Better wash up, Yank. You sleep better. Wash up, Yank. Wash up! Wash up!

YANK--[*Resentfully.*] Aw say, youse guys. Lemme alone. Can't youse see I'm tryin' to tink?

ALL--[*Repeating the word after him as one with cynical mockery.*] Think! [*The word has a brazen, metallic quality as if their throats were phonograph horns. It is followed by a chorus of hard, barking laughter.*]

YANK--[*Springing to his feet and glaring at them belligerently.*] Yes, tink! Tink, dat's what I said! What about it? [*They are silent, puzzled by his sudden resentment at what used to be one of his jokes. Yank sits down again in the same attitude of "The Thinker."*]

VOICES--Leave him alone.

He's got a grouch on.

Why wouldn't he?

PADDY--[*With a wink at the others.*] Sure I know what's the matther. 'Tis aisy to see. He's fallen in love, I'm telling you.

ALL--[*Repeating the word after him as one with cynical mockery.*] Love! [*The word has a brazen, metallic quality as if their throats were phonograph horns. It is followed by a chorus of hard, barking laughter.*]

YANK--[*With a contemptuous snort.*] Love, hell! Hate, dat's what. I've fallen in hate, get me?

PADDY--[*Philosophically*] 'Twould take a wise man to tell one from the other. [*With a bitter, ironical scorn, increasing as he goes on.*] But I'm telling you it's love that's in it. Sure what else but love for us poor bastes in the stokehole would be bringing a fine lady, dressed like a white quane, down a mile of ladders and steps to be havin' a look at us? [*A growl of anger goes up from all sides.*]

LONG--[*Jumping on a bench--hecticly*] Hinsultin' us! Hinsultin' us, the bloody cow! And them bloody engineers! What right 'as they got to be exhibitin' us 's if we was bleedin' monkeys in a menagerie? Did we sign for hinsults to our dignity as 'onest workers? Is that in the ship's articles? You kin bloody well bet it ain't! But I knows why they done it. I arsked a deck steward 'o she was and 'e told me. 'Er old man's a bleedin' millionaire, a bloody Capitalist! 'E's got enuf bloody gold to sink this bleedin' ship! 'E makes arf the bloody steel in the world! 'E owns this bloody boat! And you and me, comrades, we're 'is slaves! And the skipper and mates and engineers, they're 'is slaves! And she's 'is bloody daughter and we're all 'er slaves, too! And she gives 'er orders as 'ow she wants to see the bloody animals below decks and down they takes 'er! [*There is a roar of rage from all sides.*]

YANK--[*Blinking at him bewilderedly.*] Say! Wait a moment! Is all dat straight goods?

LONG--Straight as string! The bleedin' steward as waits on 'em, 'e told me about 'er. And what're we goin' ter do, I arsks yer? 'Ave we got ter swaller 'er hinsults like dogs? It ain't in the ship's articles. I tell yer we got a case. We kin go ter law--

YANK--[*With abysmal contempt.*] Hell! Law!

ALL--[*Repeating the word after him as one with cynical mockery.*] Law! [*The word has a brazen metallic quality as if their throats were phonograph horns. It is followed by a chorus of hard, barking laughter.*]

LONG--[*Feeling the ground slipping from under his feet--desperately.*] As voters and citizens we kin force the bloody governments--

YANK--[*With abysmal contempt.*] Hell! Governments!

ALL--[*Repeating the word after him as one with cynical mockery.*] Governments! [*The word has a brazen metallic quality as if their throats were phonograph horns. It is followed by a chorus of hard, barking laughter.*]

LONG--[*Hysterically.*] We're free and equal in the sight of God--

YANK--[*With abysmal contempt.*] Hell! God!

ALL--[*Repeating the word after him as one with cynical mockery.*] God! [*The word has a brazen metallic quality as if their throats were phonograph horns. It is followed by a chorus of hard, barking laughter.*]

YANK--[*Witheringly.*] Aw, join de Salvation Army!

ALL--Sit down! Shut up! Damn fool! Sea-lawyer! [*Long slinks back out of sight.*]

PADDY--[*Continuing the trend of his thoughts as if he had never been interrupted--bitterly.*] And there she was standing behind us, and the Second pointing at us like a man you'd hear in a circus would be saying: In this cage is a queerer kind of baboon than ever you'd find in darkest Africy. We roast them in their own sweat--and be damned if you won't hear some of thim saying they like it! [*He glances scornfully at Yank.*]

YANK--[*With a bewildered uncertain growl.*] Aw!

PADDY--And there was Yank roarin' curses and turning round wid his shovel to brain her--and she looked at him, and him at her--

YANK--[*Slowly.*] She was all white. I tought she was a ghost. Sure.

PADDY--[*With heavy, biting sarcasm.*] 'Twas love at first sight, divil a doubt of it! If you'd seen the endearin' look on her pale mug when she shrivelled away with her hands over her eyes to shut out the sight of him! Sure, 'twas as if she'd seen a great hairy ape escaped from the Zoo!

YANK--[*Stung--with a growl of rage.*] Aw!

PADDY--And the loving way Yank heaved his shovel at the skull of her, only she was out the door! [*A grin breaking over his face.*] 'Twas touching, I'm telling you! It put the touch of home, swate home in the stokehole. [*There is a roar of laughter from all.*]

YANK--[*Glaring at Paddy menacingly.*] Aw, choke dat off, see!

PADDY--[*Not heeding him--to the others.*] And her grabbin' at the Second's arm for protection. [*With a grotesque imitation of a woman's voice.*] Kiss me, Engineer dear, for it's dark down here and me old man's in Wall Street making money! Hug me tight, darlin', for I'm afeerd in the dark and me mother's on deck makin' eyes at the skipper! [*Another roar of laughter.*]

YANK--[*Threateningly.*] Say! What yuh tryin' to do, kid me, yuh old Harp?

PADDY--Divil a bit! Ain't I wishin' myself you'd brained her?

YANK--[*Fiercely.*] I'll brain her! I'll brain her yet, wait 'n' see! [*Coming over to Paddy--slowly.*] Say, is dat what she called me--a hairy ape?

PADDY--She looked it at you if she didn't say the word itself.

YANK--[*Grinning horribly.*] Hairy ape, huh? Sure! Dat's de way she
looked at me, aw right. Hairy ape! So dat's me, huh? [*Bursting into
rage--as if she were still in front of him.*] Yuh skinny tart! Yuh
white-faced bum, yuh! I'll show yuh who's a ape! [*Turning to the
others, bewilderment seizing him again.*] Say, youse guys. I was
bawlin' him out for pullin' de whistle on us. You heard me. And den I
seen youse lookin' at somep'n and I tought he'd sneaked down to come up
in back of me, and I hopped round to knock him dead wit de shovel. And
dere she was wit de light on her! Christ, yuh coulda pushed me over
with a finger! I was scared, get me? Sure! I tought she was a ghost,
see? She was all in white like dey wrap around stiffs. You seen her.
Kin yuh blame me? She didn't belong, dat's what. And den when I come to
and seen it was a real skoit and seen de way she was lookin' at
me--like Paddy said--Christ, I was sore, get me? I don't stand for dat
stuff from nobody. And I flung de shovel--on'y she'd beat it.
[*Furiously.*] I wished it'd banged her! I wished it'd knocked her
block off!

LONG--And be 'anged for murder or 'lectrocuted? She ain't bleedin' well
worth it.

YANK--I don't give a damn what! I'd be square wit her, wouldn't I? Tink
I wanter let her put somep'n over on me? Tink I'm goin' to let her git
away wit dat stuff? Yuh don't know me! Noone ain't never put nothin'
over on me and got away wit it, see!--not dat kind of stuff--no guy and
no skoit neither! I'll fix her! Maybe she'll come down again--

VOICE--No chance, Yank. You scared her out of a year's growth.

YANK--I scared her? Why de hell should I scare her? Who de hell is she?
Ain't she de same as me? Hairy ape, huh? [*With his old confident
bravado.*] I'll show her I'm better'n her, if she on'y knew it. I
belong and she don't, see! I move and she's dead! Twenty-five knots a

hour, dats me! Dat carries her but I make dat. She's on'y baggage.
Sure! [*Again bewilderedly.*] But, Christ, she was funny lookin'! Did
yuh pipe her hands? White and skinny. Yuh could see de bones trough
'em. And her mush, dat was dead white, too. And her eyes, dey was like
dey'd seen a ghost. Me, dat was! Sure! Hairy ape! Ghost, huh? Look at
dat arm! [*He extends his right arm, swelling out the great muscles.*]
I coulda took her wit dat, wit' just my little finger even, and broke
her in two. [*Again bewilderedly.*] Say, who is dat skoit, huh? What is
she? What's she come from? Who made her? Who give her de noive to look
at me like dat? Dis ting's got my goat right. I don't get her. She's
new to me. What does a skoit like her mean, huh? She don't belong, get
me! I can't see her. [*With growing anger.*] But one ting I'm wise to,
aw right, aw right! Youse all kin bet your shoits I'll git even wit
her. I'll show her if she tinks she--She grinds de organ and I'm on de
string, huh? I'll fix her! Let her come down again and I'll fling her
in de furnace! She'll move den! She won't shiver at nothin', den!
Speed, dat'll be her! She'll belong den! [*He grins horribly.*]

PADDY--She'll never come. She's had her belly-full, I'm telling you.
She'll be in bed now, I'm thinking, wid ten doctors and nurses feedin'
her salts to clean the fear out of her.

YANK--[*Enraged.*] Yuh tink I made her sick, too, do yuh? Just lookin'
at me, huh? Hairy ape, huh? [*In a frenzy of rage.*] I'll fix her! I'll
tell her where to git off! She'll git down on her knees and take it
back or I'll bust de face offen her! [*Shaking one fist upward and
beating on his chest with the other.*] I'll find yuh! I'm comin', d'yuh
hear? I'll fix yuh, God damn yuh! [*He makes a rush for the door.*]

VOICES--Stop him!

He'll get shot!

He'll murder her!

Trip him up!

Hold him!

He's gone crazy!

Gott, he's strong!

Hold him down!

Look out for a kick!

Pin his arms!

[*They have all piled on him and, after a fierce struggle, by sheer weight of numbers have borne him to the floor just inside the door.*]

PADDY--[*Who has remained detached.*] Kape him down till he's cooled off. [*Scornfully.*] Yerra, Yank, you're a great fool. Is it payin' attention at all you are to the like of that skinny sow widout one drop of rale blood in her?

YANK--[*Frenziedly, from the bottom of the heap.*] She done me doit! She done me doit, didn't she? I'll git square wit her! I'll get her some way! Git offen me, youse guys! Lemme up! I'll show her who's a ape!

[*Curtain*]

SCENE V

SCENE--Three weeks later. A corner of Fifth Avenue in the Fifties on a fine, Sunday morning. A general atmosphere of clean, well-tidied, wide street; a flood of mellow, tempered sunshine; gentle, genteel breezes. In the rear, the show windows of two shops, a jewelry establishment on the corner, a furrier's next to it. Here the adornments of extreme wealth are tantalizingly displayed. The jeweler's window is gaudy with glittering diamonds, emeralds, rubies, pearls, etc., fashioned in ornate tiaras, crowns, necklaces, collars, etc. From each piece hangs an enormous tag from which a dollar sign and numerals in intermittent electric lights wink out the incredible prices. The same in the furrier's. Rich furs of all varieties hang there bathed in a downpour of artificial light. The general effect is of a background of magnificence cheapened and made grotesque by commercialism, a background in tawdry disharmony with the clear light and sunshine on the street itself.

Up the side street Yank and Long come swaggering. Long is dressed in shore clothes, wears a black Windsor tie, cloth cap. Yank is in his dirty dungarees. A fireman's cap with black peak is cocked defiantly on the side of his head. He has not shaved for days and around his fierce, resentful eyes--as around those of Long to a lesser degree--the black smudge of coal dust still sticks like make-up. They hesitate and stand together at the corner, swaggering, looking about them with a forced, defiant contempt.

LONG--[**Indicating it all with an oratorical gesture.**] Well, 'ere we are. Fif' Avenoo. This 'ere's their bleedin' private lane, as yer might say. [**Bitterly.**] We're trespassers 'ere. Proletarians keep orf the grass!

YANK--[***Dully.***] I don't see no grass, yuh boob. [***Staring at the sidewalk.***] Clean, ain't it? Yuh could eat a fried egg offen it. The white wings got some job sweepin' dis up. [***Looking up and down the avenue--surlily.***] Where's all de white-collar stiffs yuh said was here--and de skoits--her kind?

LONG--In church, blarst 'em! Arskin' Jesus to give 'em more money.

YANK--Choich, huh? I useter go to choich onct--sure--when I was a kid. Me old man and woman, dey made me. Dey never went demselves, dough. Always got too big a head on Sunday mornin', dat was dem. [***With a grin.***] Dey was scrappers for fair, bot' of dem. On Satiday nights when dey bot' got a skinful dey could put up a bout oughter been staged at de Garden. When dey got trough dere wasn't a chair or table wit a leg under it. Or else dey bot' jumped on me for somep'n. Dat was where I loined to take punishment. [***With a grin and a swagger.***] I'm a chip offen de old block, get me?

LONG--Did yer old man follow the sea?

YANK--Naw. Worked along shore. I runned away when me old lady croaked wit de tremens. I helped at truckin' and in de market. Den I shipped in de stokehole. Sure. Dat belongs. De rest was nothin'. [***Looking around him.***] I ain't never seen dis before. De Brooklyn waterfront, dat was where I was dragged up. [***Taking a deep breath.***] Dis ain't so bad at dat, huh?

LONG--Not bad? Well, we pays for it wiv our bloody sweat, if yer wants to know!

YANK--[***With sudden angry disgust.***] Aw, hell! I don't see noone,

see--like her. All dis gives me a pain. It don't belong. Say, ain't
dere a backroom around dis dump? Let's go shoot a ball. All dis is too
clean and quiet and dolled-up, get me! It gives me a pain.

LONG--Wait and yer'll bloody well see--

YANK--I don't wait for noone. I keep on de move. Say, what yuh drag me
up here for, anyway? Tryin' to kid me, yuh simp, yuh?

LONG--Yer wants to get back at her, don't yer? That's what yer been
saying' every bloomin' 'our since she hinsulted yer.

YANK--[*Vehemently.*] Sure ting I do! Didn't I try to git even wit her
in Southampton? Didn't I sneak on de dock and wait for her by de
gangplank? I was goin' to spit in her pale mug, see! Sure, right in her
pop-eyes! Dat woulda made me even, see? But no chanct. Dere was a whole
army of plain clothes bulls around. Dey spotted me and gimme de bum's
rush. I never seen her. But I'll git square wit her yet, you watch!
[*Furiously.*] De lousey tart! She tinks she kin get away wit
moider--but not wit me! I'll fix her! I'll tink of a way!

LONG--[*As disgusted as he dares to be.*] Ain't that why I brought yer
up 'ere--to show yer? Yer been lookin' at this 'ere 'ole affair wrong.
Yer been actin' an' talkin' 's if it was all a bleedin' personal matter
between yer and that bloody cow. I wants to convince yer she was on'y a
representative of 'er clarss. I wants to awaken yer bloody clarss
consciousness. Then yer'll see it's 'er clarss yer've got to fight, not
'er alone. There's a 'ole mob of 'em like 'er, Gawd blind 'em!

YANK--[*Spitting on his hands--belligerently.*] De more de merrier when
I gits started. Bring on de gang!

LONG--Yer'll see 'em in arf a mo', when that church lets out. [*He turns and sees the window display in the two stores for the first time.*] Blimey! Look at that, will yer? [*They both walk back and stand looking in the jewelers. Long flies into a fury.*] Just look at this 'ere bloomin' mess! Just look at it! Look at the bleedin' prices on 'em--more'n our 'old bloody stokehole makes in ten voyages sweatin' in 'ell! And they--her and her bloody clarss--buys 'em for toys to dangle on 'em! One of these 'ere would buy scoff for a starvin' family for a year!

YANK--Aw, cut de sob stuff! T' hell wit de starvin' family! Yuh'll be passin' de hat to me next. [*With naive admiration.*] Say, dem tings is pretty, huh? Bet yuh dey'd hock for a piece of change aw right. [*Then turning away, bored.*] But, aw hell, what good are dey? Let her have 'em. Dey don't belong no more'n she does. [*With a gesture of sweeping the jewelers into oblivion.*] All dat don't count, get me?

LONG--[*Who has moved to the furriers--indignantly.*] And I s'pose this 'ere don't count neither--skins of poor, 'armless animals slaughtered so as 'er and 'ers can keep their bleedin' noses warm!

YANK--[*Who has been staring at something inside--with queer excitement.*] Take a slant at dat! Give it de once-over! Monkey fur--two t'ousand bucks! [*Bewilderedly.*] Is dat straight goods--monkey fur? What de hell--?

LONG--[*Bitterly.*] It's straight enuf. [*With grim humor.*] They wouldn't bloody well pay that for a 'airy ape's skin--no, nor for the 'ole livin' ape with all 'is 'ead, and body, and soul thrown in!

YANK--[*Clenching his fists, his face growing pale with rage as if the skin in the window were a personal insult.*] Trowin' it up in my face! Christ! I'll fix her!

LONG--[*Excitedly.*] Church is out. 'Ere they come, the bleedin' swine. [*After a glance at Yank's lowering face--uneasily.*] Easy goes, Comrade. Keep yer bloomin' temper. Remember force defeats itself. It ain't our weapon. We must impress our demands through peaceful means--the votes of the on-marching proletarians of the bloody world!

YANK--[*With abysmal contempt.*] Votes, hell! Votes is a joke, see. Votes for women! Let dem do it!

LONG--[*Still more uneasily.*] Calm, now. Treat 'em wiv the proper contempt. Observe the bleedin' parasites but 'old yer 'orses.

YANK--[*Angrily.*] Git away from me! Yuh're yellow, dat's what. Force, dat's me! De punch, dat's me every time, see! [*The crowd from church enter from the right, sauntering slowly and affectedly, their heads held stiffly up, looking neither to right nor left, talking in toneless, simpering voices. The women are rouged, calcimined, dyed, overdressed to the nth degree. The men are in Prince Alberts, high hats, spats, canes, etc. A procession of gaudy marionettes, yet with something of the relentless horror of Frankensteins in their detached, mechanical unawareness.*]

VOICES--Dear Doctor Caiaphas! He is so sincere!
  What was the sermon? I dozed off.
  About the radicals, my dear--and the false
  doctrines that are being preached.
  We must organize a hundred per cent American bazaar.
  And let everyone contribute one one-hundredth percent
  of their income tax.
  What an original idea!
  We can devote the proceeds to rehabilitating the veil of the

temple.

But that has been done so many times.

YANK--[*Glaring from one to the other of them--with an insulting snort of scorn.*] Huh! Huh! [*Without seeming to see him, they make wide detours to avoid the spot where he stands in the middle of the sidewalk.*]

LONG--[*Frightenedly.*] Keep yer bloomin' mouth shut, I tells yer.

YANK--[*Viciously.*] G'wan! Tell it to Sweeney! [*He swaggers away and deliberately lurches into a top-hatted gentleman, then glares at him pugnaciously.*] Say, who d'yuh tink yuh're bumpin'? Tink yuh own de oith?

GENTLEMAN--[*Coldly and affectedly.*] I beg your pardon. [*He has not looked at YANK and passes on without a glance, leaving him bewildered.*]

LONG--[*Rushing up and grabbing YANK's arm.*] 'Ere! Come away! This wasn't what I meant. Yer'll 'ave the bloody coppers down on us.

YANK--[*Savagely--giving him a push that sends him sprawling.*] G'wan!

LONG--[*Picks himself up--hysterically.*] I'll pop orf then. This ain't what I meant. And whatever 'appens, yer can't blame me. [*He slinks off left.*]

YANK--T' hell wit youse! [*He approaches a lady--with a vicious grin and a smirking wink.*] Hello, Kiddo. How's every little ting? Got anyting on for to-night? I know an old boiler down to de docks we kin crawl into. [*The lady stalks by without a look, without a change of pace. YANK turns to others--insultingly.*] Holy smokes, what a mug! Go hide yuhself before de horses shy at yuh. Gee, pipe de heinie on dat one! Say, youse, yuh look like de stoin of a ferryboat. Paint and powder! All dolled up to kill! Yuh look like stiffs laid out for de boneyard! Aw, g'wan, de lot of youse! Yuh give me de eye-ache. Yuh don't belong, get me! Look at me, why don't youse dare? I belong, dat's me! [*Pointing to a skyscraper across the street which is in process of construction--with bravado.*] See dat building goin' up dere? See de steel work? Steel, dat's me! Youse guys live on it and tink yuh're somep'n. But I'm IN it, see! I'm de hoistin' engine dat makes it go up! I'm it--de inside and bottom of it! Sure! I'm steel and steam and smoke and de rest of it! It moves--speed--twenty-five stories up--and me at de top and bottom--movin'! Youse simps don't move. Yuh're on'y dolls I winds up to see 'm spin. Yuh're de garbage, get me--de leavins--de ashes we dump over de side! Now, whata yuh gotto say? [*But as they seem neither to see nor hear him, he flies into a fury.*] Bums! Pigs! Tarts! Bitches! [*He turns in a rage on the men, bumping viciously into them but not jarring them the least bit. Rather it is he who recoils after each collision. He keeps growling.*] Git off de oith! G'wan, yuh bum! Look where yuh're goin,' can't yuh? Git outa here! Fight, why don't yuh? Put up yer mits! Don't be a dog! Fight or I'll knock yuh dead! [*But, without seeming to see him, they all answer with mechanical affected politeness:*] I beg your pardon. [*Then at a cry from one of the women, they all scurry to the furrier's window.*]

THE WOMAN--[*Ecstatically, with a gasp of delight.*] Monkey fur! [*The whole crowd of men and women chorus after her in the same tone of affected delight.*] Monkey fur!

YANK--[*With a jerk of his head back on his shoulders, as if he had received a punch full in the face--raging.*] I see yuh, all in white! I see yuh, yuh white-faced tart, yuh! Hairy ape, huh? I'll hairy ape yuh! [*He bends down and grips at the street curbing as if to pluck it out *and hurl it. Foiled in this, snarling with passion, he leaps to the lamp-post on the corner and tries to pull it up for a club. Just at that moment a bus is heard rumbling up. A fat, high-hatted, spatted gentleman runs out from the side street. He calls out plaintively: "Bus! Bus! Stop there!" and runs full tilt into the bending, straining YANK, who is bowled off his balance.*]

YANK--[*Seeing a fight--with a roar of joy as he springs to his feet.*] At last! Bus, huh? I'll bust yuh! [*He lets drive a terrific swing, his fist landing full on the fat gentleman's face. But the gentleman stands unmoved as if nothing had happened.*]

GENTLEMAN--I beg your pardon. [*Then irritably.*] You have made me lose my bus. [*He claps his hands and begins to scream:*] Officer! Officer! [*Many police whistles shrill out on the instant and a whole platoon of policemen rush in on YANK from all sides. He tries to fight but is clubbed to the pavement and fallen upon. The crowd at the window have not moved or noticed this disturbance. The clanging gong of the patrol wagon approaches with a clamoring din.*]

[*Curtain*]

SCENE VI

SCENE--Night of the following day. A row of cells in the prison on Blackwells Island. The cells extend back diagonally from right front to left rear. They do not stop, but disappear in the dark background as if they ran on, numberless, into infinity. One electric bulb from the low ceiling of the narrow corridor sheds its light through the heavy steel bars of the cell at the extreme front and reveals part of the interior. YANK can be seen within, crouched on the edge of his cot in the attitude of Rodin's "The Thinker." His face is spotted with black and blue bruises. A blood-stained bandage is wrapped around his head.

YANK--[*Suddenly starting as if awakening from a dream, reaches out and shakes the bars--aloud to himself, wonderingly.*] Steel. Dis is de Zoo, huh? [*A burst of hard, barking laughter comes from the unseen occupants of the cells, runs back down the tier, and abruptly ceases.*]

VOICES--[*Mockingly.*] The Zoo? That's a new name for this coop--a damn good name! Steel, eh? You said a mouthful. This is the old iron house. Who is that boob talkin'? He's the bloke they brung in out of his head. The bulls had beat him up fierce.

YANK--[*Dully.*] I musta been dreamin'. I tought I was in a cage at de Zoo--but de apes don't talk, do dey?

VOICES--[*With mocking laughter.*] You're in a cage aw right.

A coop!

A pen!

A sty!

A kennel! [*Hard laughter--a pause.*]

Say, guy! Who are you? No, never mind lying. What are you?

Yes, tell us your sad story. What's your game?

What did they jug yuh for?

YANK--[*Dully.*] I was a fireman--stokin' on de liners. [*Then with sudden rage, rattling his cell bars.*] I'm a hairy ape, get me? And I'll bust youse all in de jaw if yuh don't lay off kiddin' me.

VOICES--Huh! You're a hard boiled duck ain't you!

When you spit, it bounces! [*Laughter.*]

Aw, can it. He's a regular guy. Ain't you?

What did he say he was--a ape?

YANK--[*Defiantly.*] Sure ting! Ain't dat what youse all are--apes? [*A silence. Then a furious rattling of bars from down the corridor.*]

A VOICE--[*Thick with rage.*] I'll show yuh who's a ape, yuh bum!

VOICES--Ssshh! Nix!

Can de noise!

Piano!

You'll have the guard down on us!

YANK--[*Scornfully.*] De guard? Yuh mean de keeper, don't yuh? [*Angry exclamations from all the cells.*]

VOICE--[*Placatingly.*] Aw, don't pay no attention to him. He's off his nut from the beatin'-up he got. Say, you guy! We're waitin' to hear what they landed you for--or ain't yuh tellin'?

YANK--Sure, I'll tell youse. Sure! Why de hell not? On'y--youse won't get me. Nobody gets me but me, see? I started to tell de Judge and all he says was: "Toity days to tink it over." Tink it over! Christ, dat's all I been doin' for weeks! [*After a pause.*] I was tryin' to git even wit someone, see?--someone dat done me doit.

VOICES--[*Cynically.*] De old stuff, I bet. Your goil, huh?

Give yuh the double-cross, huh?

That's them every time!

Did yuh beat up de odder guy?

YANK--[*Disgustedly*] Aw, yuh're all wrong! Sure dere was a skoit in it--but not what youse mean, not dat old tripe. Dis was a new kind of skoit. She was dolled up all in white--in de stokehole. I tought she was a ghost. Sure. [*A pause.*]

VOICES--[*Whispering.*] Gee, he's still nutty.

Let him rave. It's fun listenin'.

YANK--[*Unheeding--groping in his thoughts.*] Her hands--dey was skinny and white like dey wasn't real but painted on somep'n. Dere was a million miles from me to her--twenty-five knots a hour. She was like some dead ting de cat brung in. Sure, dat's what. She didn't belong. She belonged in de window of a toy store, or on de top of a garbage can, see! Sure! [*He breaks out angrily.*] But would yuh believe it, she had de noive to do me doit. She lamped me like she was seein' somep'n broke loose from de menagerie. Christ, yuh'd oughter seen her

eyes! [*He rattles the bars of his cell furiously.*] But I'll get back
at her yet, you watch! And if I can't find her I'll take it out on de
gang she runs wit. I'm wise to where dey hangs out now. I'll show her
who belongs! I'll show her who's in de move and who ain't. You watch my
smoke!

VOICES--[*Serious and joking.*] Dat's de talkin'!

Take her for all she's got!

What was this dame, anyway? Who was she, eh?

YANK--I dunno. First cabin stiff. Her old man's a millionaire, dey
says--name of Douglas.

VOICES--Douglas? That's the president of the Steel Trust, I bet.

Sure. I seen his mug in de papers.

He's filthy with dough.

VOICE--Hey, feller, take a tip from me. If you want to get back at that
dame, you better join the Wobblies. You'll get some action then.

YANK--Wobblies? What de hell's dat?

VOICE--Ain't you ever heard of the I. W. W.?

YANK--Naw. What is it?

VOICE--A gang of blokes--a tough gang. I been readin' about 'em to-day
in the paper. The guard give me the Sunday Times. There's a long spiel
about 'em. It's from a speech made in the Senate by a guy named Senator

Queen. [*He is in the cell next to YANK's. There is a rustling of paper.*] Wait'll I see if I got light enough and I'll read you. Listen. [*He reads:*] "There is a menace existing in this country to-day which threatens the vitals of our fair Republic--as foul a menace against the very life-blood of the American Eagle as was the foul conspiracy of Cataline against the eagles of ancient Rome!"

VOICE [*Disgustedly.*] Aw hell! Tell him to salt de tail of dat eagle!

VOICE--[*Reading:*] "I refer to that devil's brew of rascals, jailbirds, murderers and cutthroats who libel all honest working men by calling themselves the Industrial Workers of the World; but in the light of their nefarious plots, I call them the Industrious WRECKERS of the World!"

YANK--[*With vengeful satisfaction.*] Wreckers, dat's de right dope! Dat belongs! Me for dem!

VOICE--Ssshh! [*Reading.*] "This fiendish organization is a foul ulcer on the fair body of our Democracy--"

VOICE--Democracy, hell! Give him the boid, fellers--the raspberry! [*They do.*]

VOICE--Ssshh! [*Reading:*] "Like Cato I say to this senate, the I. W. W. must be destroyed! For they represent an ever-present dagger pointed at the heart of the greatest nation the world has ever known, where all men are born free and equal, with equal opportunities to all, where the Founding Fathers have guaranteed to each one happiness, where Truth, Honor, Liberty, Justice, and the Brotherhood of Man are a religion absorbed with one's mother's milk, taught at our father's knee, sealed, signed, and stamped upon in the glorious Constitution of these United States!" [*A perfect storm of hisses, catcalls, boos, and hard laughter.*]

VOICES--[*Scornfully.*] Hurrah for de Fort' of July!

Pass de hat!

Liberty!

Justice!

Honor!

Opportunity!

Brotherhood!

ALL--[*With abysmal scorn.*] Aw, hell!

VOICE--Give that Queen Senator guy the bark! All togedder now--one--two--tree--[*A terrific chorus of barking and yapping.*]

GUARD--[*From a distance.*] Quiet there, youse--or I'll git the hose. [*The noise subsides.*]

YANK--[*With growling rage.*] I'd like to catch dat senator guy alone for a second. I'd loin him some trute!

VOICE--Ssshh! Here's where he gits down to cases on the Wobblies. [*Reads:*] "They plot with fire in one hand and dynamite in the other. They stop not before murder to gain their ends, nor at the outraging of defenceless womanhood. They would tear down society, put the lowest scum in the seats of the mighty, turn Almighty God's revealed plan for the world topsy-turvy, and make of our sweet and lovely civilization a shambles, a desolation where man, God's masterpiece, would soon degenerate back to the ape!"

VOICE--[*To YANK.*] Hey, you guy. There's your ape stuff again.

YANK--[*With a growl of fury.*] I got him. So dey blow up tings, do dey? Dey turn tings round, do dey? Hey, lend me dat paper, will yuh?

VOICE--Sure. Give it to him. On'y keep it to yourself, see. We don't wanter listen to no more of that slop.

VOICE--Here you are. Hide it under your mattress.

YANK--[*Reaching out.*] Tanks. I can't read much but I kin manage. [*He sits, the paper in the hand at his side, in the attitude of Rodin's "The Thinker." A pause. Several snores from down the corridor. Suddenly YANK jumps to his feet with a furious groan as if some appalling thought had crashed on him--bewilderedly.*] Sure--her old man--president of de Steel Trust--makes half de steel in de world--steel--where I tought I belonged--drivin' trou--movin'--in dat--to make HER--and cage me in for her to spit on! Christ [*He shakes the bars of his cell door till the whole tier trembles. Irritated, protesting exclamations from those awakened or trying to get to sleep.*] He made dis--dis cage! Steel! IT don't belong, dat's what! Cages, cells, locks, bolts, bars--dat's what it means!--holdin' me down wit him at de top! But I'll drive trou! Fire, dat melts it! I'll be fire--under de heap--fire dat never goes out--hot as hell--breakin' out in de night--[*While he has been saying this last he has shaken his cell door to a clanging accompaniment. As he comes to the "breakin' out" he seizes one bar with both hands and, putting his two feet up against the others so that his position is parallel to the floor like a monkey's, he gives a great wrench backwards. The bar bends like a licorice stick under his tremendous strength. Just at this moment the PRISON GUARD rushes in, dragging a hose behind him.*]

GUARD--[*Angrily.*] I'll loin youse bums to wake me up! [*Sees YANK.*] Hello, it's you, huh? Got the D.T.s, hey? Well, I'll cure 'em. I'll drown your snakes for yuh! [*Noticing the bar.*] Hell, look at dat bar bended! On'y a bug is strong enough for dat!

YANK--[*Glaring at him.*] Or a hairy ape, yuh big yellow bum! Look out! Here I come! [*He grabs another bar.*]

GUARD--[*Scared now--yelling off left.*] Toin de hoose on, Ben!--full pressure! And call de others--and a strait jacket! [*The curtain is falling. As it hides YANK from view, there is a splattering smash as the stream of water hits the steel of YANK's cell.*]

[*Curtain*]

SCENE VII

SCENE--Nearly a month later. An I. W. W. local near the waterfront, showing the interior of a front room on the ground floor, and the street outside. Moonlight on the narrow street, buildings massed in black shadow. The interior of the room, which is general assembly room, office, and reading room, resembles some dingy settlement boys club. A desk and high stool are in one corner. A table with papers, stacks of pamphlets, chairs about it, is at center. The whole is decidedly cheap, banal, commonplace and unmysterious as a room could well be. The secretary is perched on the stool making entries in a large ledger. An eye shade casts his face into shadows. Eight or ten men, longshoremen, iron workers, and the like, are grouped about the table. Two are playing checkers. One is writing a letter. Most of them are smoking pipes. A big signboard is on the wall at the rear, "Industrial Workers of the World--Local No. 57."

YANK--[*Comes down the street outside. He is dressed as in Scene Five. He moves cautiously, mysteriously. He comes to a point opposite the door; tiptoes softly up to it, listens, is impressed by the silence within, knocks carefully, as if he were guessing at the password to some secret rite. Listens. No answer. Knocks again a bit louder. No answer. Knocks impatiently, much louder.*]

SECRETARY--[*Turning around on his stool.*] What the devil is that--someone knocking? [*Shouts:*] Come in, why don't you? [*All the men in the room look up. YANK opens the door slowly, gingerly, as if afraid of an ambush. He looks around for secret doors, mystery, is taken aback by the commonplaceness of the room and the men in it, thinks he may have gotten in the wrong place, then sees the signboard on the wall and is reassured.*]

YANK--[*Blurts out.*] Hello.

MEN--[*Reservedly.*] Hello.

YANK--[*More easily.*] I tought I'd bumped into de wrong dump.

SECRETARY--[*Scrutinizing him carefully.*] Maybe you have. Are you a member?

YANK--Naw, not yet. Dat's what I come for--to join.

SECRETARY--That's easy. What's your job--longshore?

YANK--Naw. Fireman--stoker on de liners.

SECRETARY--[*With satisfaction.*] Welcome to our city. Glad to know you people are waking up at last. We haven't got many members in your line.

YANK--Naw. Dey're all dead to de woild.

SECRETARY--Well, you can help to wake 'em. What's your name? I'll make out your card.

YANK--[*Confused.*] Name? Lemme tink.

SECRETARY--[*Sharply.*] Don't you know your own name?

YANK--Sure; but I been just Yank for so long--Bob, dat's it--Bob Smith.

SECRETARY--[*Writing.*] Robert Smith. [*Fills out the rest of card.*] Here you are. Cost you half a dollar.

YANK--Is dat all--four bits? Dat's easy. [*Gives the SECRETARY the money.*]

SECRETARY--[*Throwing it in drawer.*] Thanks. Well, make yourself at home. No introductions needed. There's literature on the table. Take some of those pamphlets with you to distribute aboard ship. They may bring results. Sow the seed, only go about it right. Don't get caught and fired. We got plenty out of work. What we need is men who can hold their jobs--and work for us at the same time.

YANK--Sure. [*But he still stands, embarrassed and uneasy.*]

SECRETARY--[*Looking at him--curiously.*] What did you knock for? Think we had a coon in uniform to open doors?

YANK--Naw. I tought it was locked--and dat yuh'd wanter give me the once-over trou a peep-hole or somep'n to see if I was right.

SECRETARY--[*Alert and suspicious but with an easy laugh.*] Think we were running a crap game? That door is never locked. What put that in your nut?

YANK--[*With a knowing grin, convinced that this is all camouflage, a part of the secrecy.*] Dis burg is full of bulls, ain't it?

SECRETARY--[*Sharply.*] What have the cops got to do with us? We're breaking no laws.

YANK--[*With a knowing wink.*] Sure. Youse wouldn't for woilds. Sure. I'm wise to dat.

SECRETARY--You seem to be wise to a lot of stuff none of us knows about.

YANK--[*With another wink.*] Aw, dat's aw right, see. [*Then made a bit resentful by the suspicious glances from all sides.*] Aw, can it! Youse needn't put me trou de toid degree. Can't youse see I belong? Sure! I'm reg'lar. I'll stick, get me? I'll shoot de woiks for youse. Dat's why I wanted to join in.

SECRETARY--[*Breezily, feeling him out.*] That's the right spirit. Only are you sure you understand what you've joined? It's all plain and above board; still, some guys get a wrong slant on us. [*Sharply.*] What's your notion of the purpose of the I. W. W.?

YANK--Aw, I know all about it.

SECRETARY--[*Sarcastically.*] Well, give us some of your valuable information.

YANK--[*Cunningly.*] I know enough not to speak outa my toin. [*Then resentfully again.*] Aw, say! I'm reg'lar. I'm wise to de game. I know yuh got to watch your step wit a stranger. For all youse know, I might be a plain-clothes dick, or somep'n, dat's what yuh're tinkin', huh? Aw, forget it! I belong, see? Ask any guy down to de docks if I don't.

SECRETARY--Who said you didn't?

YANK--After I'm 'nitiated, I'll show yuh.

SECRETARY--[*Astounded.*] Initiated? There's no initiation.

YANK--[*Disappointed.*] Ain't there no password--no grip nor nothin'?

SECRETARY--What'd you think this is--the Elks--or the Black Hand?

YANK--De Elks, hell! De Black Hand, dey're a lot of yellow backstickin' Ginees. Naw. Dis is a man's gang, ain't it?

SECRETARY--You said it! That's why we stand on our two feet in the open. We got no secrets.

YANK--[*Surprised but admiringly.*] Yuh mean to say yuh always run wide open--like dis?

SECRETARY--Exactly.

YANK--Den yuh sure got your noive wit youse!

SECRETARY--[*Sharply.*] Just what was it made you want to join us? Come out with that straight.

YANK--Yuh call me? Well, I got noive, too! Here's my hand. Yuh wanter blow tings up, don't yuh? Well, dat's me! I belong!

SECRETARY--[*With pretended carelessness.*] You mean change the unequal conditions of society by legitimate direct action--or with dynamite?

YANK--Dynamite! Blow it offen de oith--steel--all de cages--all de factories, steamers, buildings, jails--de Steel Trust and all dat makes it go.

SECRETARY--So--that's your idea, eh? And did you have any special job in that line you wanted to propose to us. [*He makes a sign to the men, who get up cautiously one by one and group behind YANK.*]

YANK--[*Boldly.*] Sure, I'll come out wit it. I'll show youse I'm one of de gang. Dere's dat millionaire guy, Douglas--

SECRETARY--President of the Steel Trust, you mean? Do you want to assassinate him?

YANK--Naw, dat don't get yuh nothin'. I mean blow up de factory, de woiks, where he makes de steel. Dat's what I'm after--to blow up de steel, knock all de steel in de woild up to de moon. Dat'll fix tings! [*Eagerly, with a touch of bravado.*] I'll do it by me lonesome! I'll show yuh! Tell me where his woiks is, how to git there, all de dope. Gimme de stuff, de old butter--and watch me do de rest! Watch de smoke and see it move! I don't give a damn if dey nab me--long as it's done! I'll soive life for it--and give 'em de laugh! [*Half to himself.*] And

I'll write her a letter and tell her de hairy ape done it. Dat'll
square tings.

SECRETARY--[*Stepping away from YANK.*] Very interesting. [*He gives a
signal. The men, huskies all, throw themselves on YANK and before he
knows it they have his legs and arms pinioned. But he is too
flabbergasted to make a struggle, anyway. They feel him over for
weapons.*]

MAN--No gat, no knife. Shall we give him what's what and put the boots
to him?

SECRETARY--No. He isn't worth the trouble we'd get into. He's too
stupid. [*He comes closer and laughs mockingly in YANK'S face.*] Ho-ho!
By God, this is the biggest joke they've put up on us yet. Hey, you
Joke! Who sent you--Burns or Pinkerton? No, by God, you're such a
bonehead I'll bet you're in the Secret Service! Well, you dirty spy,
you rotten agent provocator, you can go back and tell whatever skunk is
paying you blood-money for betraying your brothers that he's wasting
his coin. You couldn't catch a cold. And tell him that all he'll ever
get on us, or ever has got, is just his own sneaking plots that he's
framed up to put us in jail. We are what our manifesto says we are,
neither more or less--and we'll give him a copy of that any time he
calls. And as for you--[*He glares scornfully at YANK, who is sunk in
an oblivious stupor.*] Oh, hell, what's the use of talking? You're a
brainless ape.

YANK--[*Aroused by the word to fierce but futile struggles.*] What's
dat, yuh Sheeny bum, yuh!

SECRETARY--Throw him out, boys. [*In spite of his struggles, this is
done with gusto and eclat. Propelled by several parting kicks, YANK*]

lands sprawling in the middle of the narrow cobbled street. With a growl he starts to get up and storm the closed door, but stops bewildered by the confusion in his brain, pathetically impotent. He sits there, brooding, in as near to the attitude of Rodin's "Thinker" as he can get in his position.]

YANK--[*Bitterly.*] So dem boids don't tink I belong, neider. Aw, to hell wit 'em! Dey're in de wrong pew--de same old bull--soapboxes and Salvation Army--no guts! Cut out an hour offen de job a day and make me happy! Gimme a dollar more a day and make me happy! Tree square a day, and cauliflowers in de front yard--ekal rights--a woman and kids--a lousey vote--and I'm all fixed for Jesus, huh? Aw, hell! What does dat get yuh? Dis ting's in your inside, but it ain't your belly. Feedin' your face--sinkers and coffee--dat don't touch it. It's way down--at de bottom. Yuh can't grab it, and yuh can't stop it. It moves, and everyting moves. It stops and de whole woild stops. Dat's me now--I don't tick, see?--I'm a busted Ingersoll, dat's what. Steel was me, and I owned de woild. Now I ain't steel, and de woild owns me. Aw, hell! I can't see--it's all dark, get me? It's all wrong! [*He turns a bitter mocking face up like an ape gibbering at the moon.*] Say, youse up dere, Man in de Moon, yuh look so wise, gimme de answer, huh? Slip me de inside dope, de information right from de stable--where do I get off at, huh?

A POLICEMAN--[*Who has come up the street in time to hear this last--with grim humor.*] You'll get off at the station, you boob, if you don't get up out of that and keep movin'.

YANK--[*Looking up at him--with a hard, bitter laugh.*] Sure! Lock me up! Put me in a cage! Dat's de on'y answer yuh know. G'wan, lock me up!

POLICEMAN--What you been doin'?

YANK--Enuf to gimme life for! I was born, see? Sure, dat's de charge. Write it in de blotter. I was born, get me!

POLICEMAN--[*Jocosely.*] God pity your old woman! [*Then matter-of-fact.*] But I've no time for kidding. You're soused. I'd run you in but it's too long a walk to the station. Come on now, get up, or I'll fan your ears with this club. Beat it now! [*He hauls YANK to his feet.*]

YANK--[*In a vague mocking tone.*] Say, where do I go from here?

POLICEMAN--[*Giving him a push--with a grin, indifferently.*] Go to hell.

[*Curtain*]

SCENE VIII

SCENE--Twilight of the next day. The monkey house at the Zoo. One spot of clear gray light falls on the front of one cage so that the interior can be seen. The other cages are vague, shrouded in shadow from which chatterings pitched in a conversational tone can be heard. On the one cage a sign from which the word "gorilla" stands out. The gigantic animal himself is seen squatting on his haunches on a bench in much the same attitude as Rodin's "Thinker." YANK enters from the left. Immediately a chorus of angry chattering and screeching breaks out. The gorilla turns his eyes but makes no sound or move.

YANK--[*With a hard, bitter laugh.*] Welcome to your city, huh? Hail, hail, de gang's all here! [*At the sound of his voice the chattering dies away into an attentive silence. YANK walks up to the gorilla's cage and, leaning over the railing, stares in at its occupant, who stares back at him, silent and motionless. There is a pause of dead stillness. Then YANK begins to talk in a friendly confidential tone, half-mockingly, but with a deep undercurrent of sympathy.*] Say, yuh're some hard-lookin' guy, ain't yuh? I seen lots of tough nuts dat de gang called gorillas, but yuh're de foist real one I ever seen. Some chest yuh got, and shoulders, and dem arms and mits! I bet yuh got a punch in eider fist dat'd knock 'em all silly! [*This with genuine admiration. The gorilla, as if he understood, stands upright, swelling out his chest and pounding on it with his fist. YANK grins sympathetically.*] Sure, I get yuh. Yuh challenge de whole woild, huh? Yuh got what I was sayin' even if yuh muffed de woids. [*Then bitterness creeping in.*] And why wouldn't yuh get me? Ain't we both members of de same club--de Hairy Apes? [*They stare at each other--a pause--then YANK goes on slowly and bitterly.*] So yuh're what she seen when she looked at me, de white-faced tart! I was you to her, get me? On'y outa de cage--broke out--free to moider her, see? Sure! Dat's what she tought. She wasn't wise dat I was in a cage, too--worser'n yours--sure--a damn sight--'cause you got some chanct to bust loose--but me--[*He grows confused.*] Aw, hell! It's all wrong, ain't it? [*A pause.*] I s'pose yuh wanter know what I'm doin' here, huh? I been warmin' a bench down to de Battery--ever since last night. Sure. I seen de sun come up. Dat was pretty, too--all red and pink and green. I was lookin' at de skyscrapers--steel--and all de ships comin' in, sailin' out, all over de oith--and dey was steel, too. De sun was warm, dey wasn't no clouds, and dere was a breeze blowin'. Sure, it was great stuff. I got it aw right--what Paddy said about dat bein' de right dope--on'y I couldn't get IN it, see? I couldn't belong in dat. It was over my head. And I kept tinkin'--and den I beat it up here to see what youse was like. And I waited till dey was all gone to git yuh alone. Say, how d'yuh feel sittin' in dat pen all de time, havin' to stand for 'em comin' and starin' at yuh--de white-faced, skinny tarts and de boobs what marry 'em--makin' fun of yuh, laughin' at yuh, gittin' scared of yuh--damn 'em! [*He pounds on the rail with his fist. The gorilla rattles the bars of his cage and snarls. All the other monkeys set up an angry chattering in the darkness. YANK goes on excitedly.*] Sure! Dat's de way it hits me, too. On'y yuh're lucky, see? Yuh don't belong wit 'em and yuh know it. But me, I belong wit 'em--but I don't, see? Dey don't belong wit me, dat's what. Get me? Tinkin' is hard--[*He passes one hand across his forehead with a painful gesture. The gorilla growls impatiently. YANK goes on gropingly.*] It's dis way, what I'm drivin' at. Youse can sit and dope dream in de past, green woods, de jungle and de rest of it. Den yuh belong and dey don't. Den yuh kin laugh at 'em, see? Yuh're de champ of de woild. But me--I ain't got no past to tink in, nor nothin' dat's comin', on'y what's now--and dat don't belong. Sure, you're de best off! Yuh can't tink, can yuh? Yuh can't talk neider. But I kin make a bluff at talkin' and tinkin'--a'most git away wit it--a'most!--and dat's where de joker comes in. [*He laughs.*] I ain't on oith and I ain't in heaven, get me? I'm in de middle tryin' to separate 'em, takin' all de woist punches from bot' of 'em. Maybe dat's what dey call hell, huh? But you, yuh're at de bottom. You belong! Sure! Yuh're de on'y one in de woild dat does, yuh lucky stiff! [*The gorilla growls proudly.*] And dat's why dey gotter put yuh in a cage, see? [*The gorilla roars angrily.*] Sure! Yuh get me. It beats it when you try to tink it or talk it--it's way down--deep--behind--you 'n' me we feel it. Sure! Bot' members of dis club! [*He laughs--then in a savage tone.*] What de hell! T' hell wit it! A little action, dat's our meat! Dat belongs! Knock 'em down and keep bustin' 'em till dey croaks yuh wit a gat--wit steel! Sure! Are yuh game? Dey've looked at youse, ain't dey--in a cage? Wanter git even? Wanter wind up like a sport 'stead of croakin' slow in dere? [*The gorilla roars an emphatic affirmative. YANK goes on with a sort of furious exaltation.*] Sure! Yuh're reg'lar! Yuh'll stick to de finish! Me 'n' you, huh?--bot' members of this club! We'll put up one last star bout dat'll knock 'em offen deir seats! Dey'll have to make de cages stronger after we're trou! [*The gorilla is straining at his bars, growling, hopping from one foot to the other. YANK takes a jimmy from under his coat and forces the lock on the cage door. He throws this open.*] Pardon from de governor! Step out and shake hands! I'll take yuh for a walk down Fif' Avenoo. We'll knock 'em offen de oith and croak wit de band playin'. Come on, Brother. [*The gorilla scrambles gingerly out of his cage. Goes to YANK and stands looking at him. YANK keeps his mocking tone--holds out his hand.*] Shake--de secret grip of our order. [*Something, the tone of mockery, perhaps, suddenly enrages the animal. With a spring he wraps his huge arms around YANK in a murderous hug. There is a crackling snap of crushed ribs--a gasping cry, still mocking, from YANK.*] Hey, I didn't say, kiss me. [*The gorilla lets the crushed body slip to the floor; stands over it uncertainly, considering; then picks it up, throws it in the cage, shuts the door, and shuffles off menacingly into the darkness at left. A great uproar of frightened chattering and whimpering comes from the other cages. Then YANK moves, groaning, opening his eyes, and there is silence. He mutters painfully.*] Say--dey oughter match him--wit Zybszko. He got me, aw right. I'm trou. Even him didn't tink I belonged. [*Then, with sudden passionate despair.*] Christ, where do I get off at? Where do I fit in? [*Checking himself as suddenly.*] Aw, what de hell! No squakin', see! No quittin', get me! Croak wit your boots on! [*He grabs hold of the bars of the cage and hauls himself painfully to his feet--looks around him bewilderedly--forces a mocking laugh.*] In de cage, huh? [*In the strident tones of a circus barker.*] Ladies and gents, step forward and take a slant at de one and only--[*His voice *weakening*]--one and original--Hairy Ape from de wilds of--[*He slips in a heap on the floor and dies. The monkeys set up a chattering, whimpering wail. And, perhaps, the Hairy Ape at last belongs.*]

[*Curtain*]

The Codes Of Hammurabi And Moses
W. W. Davies

QTY

The discovery of the Hammurabi Code is one of the greatest achievements of archaeology, and is of paramount interest, not only to the student of the Bible, but also to all those interested in ancient history...

Religion   **ISBN:** *1-59462-338-4*   **Pages:132**
MSRP $12.95

The Theory of Moral Sentiments
Adam Smith

QTY

This work from 1749. contains original theories of conscience amd moral judgment and it is the foundation for systemof morals.

Philosophy ISBN: *1-59462-777-0*   **Pages:536**
MSRP $19.95

Jessica's First Prayer
Hesba Stretton

QTY

In a screened and secluded corner of one of the many railway-bridges which span the streets of London there could be seen a few years ago, from five o'clock every morning until half past eight, a tidily set-out coffee-stall, consisting of a trestle and board, upon which stood two large tin cans, with a small fire of charcoal burning under each so as to keep the coffee boiling during the early hours of the morning when the work-people were thronging into the city on their way to their daily toil...

Childrens   ISBN: *1-59462-373-2*   **Pages:84**
MSRP $9.95

My Life and Work
Henry Ford

QTY

Henry Ford revolutionized the world with his implementation of mass production for the Model T automobile. Gain valuable business insight into his life and work with his own auto-biography... "We have only started on our development of our country we have not as yet, with all our talk of wonderful progress, done more than scratch the surface. The progress has been wonderful enough but..."

Biographies/   ISBN: *1-59462-198-5*   **Pages:300**
MSRP $21.95

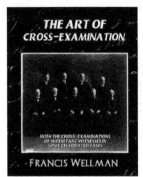

The Art of Cross-Examination
Francis Wellman

QTY

I presume it is the experience of every author, after his first book is published upon an important subject, to be almost overwhelmed with a wealth of ideas and illustrations which could readily have been included in his book, and which to his own mind, at least, seem to make a second edition inevitable. Such certainly was the case with me; and when the first edition had reached its sixth impression in five months, I rejoiced to learn that it seemed to my publishers that the book had met with a sufficiently favorable reception to justify a second and considerably enlarged edition. ..

Pages:412

Reference   ISBN: *1-59462-647-2*   *MSRP $19.95*

On the Duty of Civil Disobedience
Henry David Thoreau

QTY

Thoreau wrote his famous essay, On the Duty of Civil Disobedience, as a protest against an unjust but popular war and the immoral but popular institution of slave-owning. He did more than write—he declined to pay his taxes, and was hauled off to gaol in consequence. Who can say how much this refusal of his hastened the end of the war and of slavery ?

Law   ISBN: *1-59462-747-9*   **Pages:48**

MSRP $7.45

Dream Psychology Psychoanalysis for Beginners
Sigmund Freud

QTY

Sigmund Freud, born Sigismund Schlomo Freud (May 6, 1856 - September 23, 1939), was a Jewish-Austrian neurologist and psychiatrist who co-founded the psychoanalytic school of psychology. Freud is best known for his theories of the unconscious mind, especially involving the mechanism of repression; his redefinition of sexual desire as mobile and directed towards a wide variety of objects; and his therapeutic techniques, especially his understanding of transference in the therapeutic relationship and the presumed value of dreams as sources of insight into unconscious desires.

Pages:196

Psychology   ISBN: *1-59462-905-6*   *MSRP $15.45*

The Miracle of Right Thought
Orison Swett Marden

QTY

Believe with all of your heart that you will do what you were made to do. When the mind has once formed the habit of holding cheerful, happy, prosperous pictures, it will not be easy to form the opposite habit. It does not matter how improbable or how far away this realization may see, or how dark the prospects may be, if we visualize them as best we can, as vividly as possible, hold tenaciously to them and vigorously struggle to attain them, they will gradually become actualized, realized in the life. But a desire, a longing without endeavor, a yearning abandoned or held indifferently will vanish without realization.

Pages:360

Self Help   ISBN: *1-59462-644-8*   *MSRP $25.45*

The Rosicrucian Cosmo-Conception Mystic Christianity *by Max Heindel* ISBN: *1-59462-188-8* **$38.95**
The Rosicrucian Cosmo-conception is not dogmatic, neither does it appeal to any other authority than the reason of the student. It is: not controversial, but is: sent forth in the, hope that it may help to clear... New Age/Religion Pages 646

Abandonment To Divine Providence *by Jean-Pierre de Caussade* ISBN: *1-59462-228-0* **$25.95**
"The Rev. Jean Pierre de Caussade was one of the most remarkable spiritual writers of the Society of Jesus in France in the 18th Century. His death took place at Toulouse in 1751. His works have gone through many editions and have been republished... Inspirational/Religion Pages 400

Mental Chemistry *by Charles Haanel* ISBN: *1-59462-192-6* **$23.95**
Mental Chemistry allows the change of material conditions by combining and appropriately utilizing the power of the mind. Much like applied chemistry creates something new and unique out of careful combinations of chemicals the mastery of mental chemistry... New Age Pages 354

The Letters of Robert Browning and Elizabeth Barret Barrett 1845-1846 vol II ISBN: *1-59462-193-4* **$35.95**
by Robert Browning and Elizabeth Barrett Biographies Pages 596

Gleanings In Genesis (volume I) *by Arthur W. Pink* ISBN: *1-59462-130-6* **$27.45**
Appropriately has Genesis been termed "the seed plot of the Bible" for in it we have, in germ form, almost all of the great doctrines which are afterwards fully developed in the books of Scripture which follow... Religion/Inspirational Pages 420

The Master Key *by L. W. de Laurence* ISBN: *1-59462-001-6* **$30.95**
In no branch of human knowledge has there been a more lively increase of the spirit of research during the past few years than in the study of Psychology, Concentration and Mental Discipline. The requests for authentic lessons in Thought Control, Mental Discipline and... New Age/Business Pages 422

The Lesser Key Of Solomon Goetia *by L. W. de Laurence* ISBN: *1-59462-092-X* **$9.95**
This translation of the first book of the "Lernegton" which is now for the first time made accessible to students of Talismanic Magic was done, after careful collation and edition, from numerous Ancient Manuscripts in Hebrew, Latin, and French... New Age/Occult Pages 92

Rubaiyat Of Omar Khayyam *by Edward Fitzgerald* ISBN:*1-59462-332-5* **$13.95**
Edward Fitzgerald, whom the world has already learned, in spite of his own efforts to remain within the shadow of anonymity, to look upon as one of the rarest poets of the century, was born at Bredfield, in Suffolk, on the 31st of March, 1809. He was the third son of John Purcell... Music Pages 172

Ancient Law *by Henry Maine* ISBN: *1-59462-128-4* **$29.95**
The chief object of the following pages is to indicate some of the earliest ideas of mankind, as they are reflected in Ancient Law, and to point out the relation of those ideas to modern thought. Religion/History Pages 452

Far-Away Stories *by William J. Locke* ISBN: *1-59462-129-2* **$19.45**
"Good wine needs no bush, but a collection of mixed vintages does. And this book is just such a collection. Some of the stories I do not want to remain buried for ever in the museum files of dead magazine-numbers an author's not unpardonable vanity..." Fiction Pages 272

Life of David Crockett *by David Crockett* ISBN: *1-59462-250-7* **$27.45**
"Colonel David Crockett was one of the most remarkable men of the times in which he lived. Born in humble life, but gifted with a strong will, an indomitable courage, and unremitting perseverance... Biographies/New Age Pages 424

Lip-Reading *by Edward Nitchie* ISBN: *1-59462-206-X* **$25.95**
Edward B. Nitchie, founder of the New York School for the Hard of Hearing, now the Nitchie School of Lip-Reading, Inc, wrote "LIP-READING Principles and Practice". The development and perfecting of this meritorious work on lip-reading was an undertaking... How-to Pages 400

A Handbook of Suggestive Therapeutics, Applied Hypnotism, Psychic Science ISBN: *1-59462-214-0* **$24.95**
by Henry Munro Health/New Age/Health/Self-help Pages 376

A Doll's House: and Two Other Plays *by Henrik Ibsen* ISBN: *1-59462-112-8* **$19.95**
Henrik Ibsen created this classic when in revolutionary 1848 Rome. Introducing some striking concepts in playwriting for the realist genre, this play has been studied the world over. Fiction/Classics/Plays 308

The Light of Asia *by sir Edwin Arnold* ISBN: *1-59462-204-3* **$13.95**
In this poetic masterpiece, Edwin Arnold describes the life and teachings of Buddha. The man who was to become known as Buddha to the world was born as Prince Gautama of India but he rejected the worldly riches and abandoned the reigns of power when... Religion/History/Biographies Pages 170

The Complete Works of Guy de Maupassant *by Guy de Maupassant* ISBN: *1-59462-157-8* **$16.95**
"For days and days, nights and nights, I had dreamed of that first kiss which was to consecrate our engagement, and I knew not on what spot I should put my lips..." Fiction/Classics Pages 240

The Art of Cross-Examination *by Francis L. Wellman* ISBN: *1-59462-309-0* **$26.95**
Written by a renowned trial lawyer, Wellman imparts his experience and uses case studies to explain how to use psychology to extract desired information through questioning. How-to/Science/Reference Pages 408

Answered or Unanswered? *by Louisa Vaughan* ISBN: *1-59462-248-5* **$10.95**
Miracles of Faith in China Religion Pages 112

The Edinburgh Lectures on Mental Science (1909) *by Thomas* ISBN: *1-59462-008-3* **$11.95**
This book contains the substance of a course of lectures recently given by the writer in the Queen Street Hall, Edinburgh. Its purpose is to indicate the Natural Principles governing the relation between Mental Action and Material Conditions... New Age/Psychology Pages 148

Ayesha *by H. Rider Haggard* ISBN: *1-59462-301-5* **$24.95**
Verily and indeed it is the unexpected that happens! Probably if there was one person upon the earth from whom the Editor of this, and of a certain previous history, did not expect to hear again... Classics Pages 380

Ayala's Angel *by Anthony Trollope* ISBN: *1-59462-352-X* **$29.95**
The two girls were both pretty, but Lucy who was twenty-one who supposed to be simple and comparatively unattractive, whereas Ayala was credited, as her Bombwhat romantic name might show, with poetic charm and a taste for romance. Ayala when her father died was nineteen... Fiction Pages 484

The American Commonwealth *by James Bryce* ISBN: *1-59462-286-8* **$34.45**
An interpretation of American democratic political theory. It examines political mechanics and society from the perspective of Scotsman James Bryce Politics Pages 572

Stories of the Pilgrims *by Margaret P. Pumphrey* ISBN: *1-59462-116-0* **$17.95**
This book explores pilgrims religious oppression in England as well as their escape to Holland and eventual crossing to America on the Mayflower, and their early days in New England... History Pages 268

QTY

The Fasting Cure *by Sinclair Upton*   ISBN: *1-59462-222-1* **$13.95**
In the Cosmopolitan Magazine for May, 1910, and in the Contemporary Review (London) for April, 1910, I published an article dealing with my experiences in fasting. I have written a great many magazine articles, but never one which attracted so much attention... New Age/Self Help/Health Pages 164

Hebrew Astrology *by Sepharial*   ISBN: *1-59462-308-2* **$13.45**
In these days of advanced thinking it is a matter of common observation that we have left many of the old landmarks behind and that we are now pressing forward to greater heights and to a wider horizon than that which represented the mind-content of our progenitors...   Astrology Pages 144

Thought Vibration or The Law of Attraction in the Thought World   ISBN: *1-59462-127-6* **$12.95**

by William Walker Atkinson   Psychology/Religion Pages 144

Optimism *by Helen Keller*   ISBN: *1-59462-108-X* **$15.95**
Helen Keller was blind, deaf, and mute since 19 months old, yet famously learned how to overcome these handicaps, communicate with the world, and spread her lectures promoting optimism. An inspiring read for everyone...   Biographies/Inspirational Pages 84

Sara Crewe *by Frances Burnett*   ISBN: *1-59462-360-0* **$9.45**
In the first place, Miss Minchin lived in London. Her home was a large, dull, tall one, in a large, dull square, where all the houses were alike, and all the sparrows were alike, and where all the door-knockers made the same heavy sound...   Childrens/Classic Pages 88

The Autobiography of Benjamin Franklin *by Benjamin Franklin*   ISBN: *1-59462-135-7* **$24.95**
The Autobiography of Benjamin Franklin has probably been more extensively read than any other American historical work, and no other book of its kind has had such ups and downs of fortune. Franklin lived for many years in England, where he was agent...   Biographies/History Pages 332

Name	
Email	
Telephone	
Address	
City, State ZIP	

☐ **Credit Card**   ☐ **Check / Money Order**

Credit Card Number	
Expiration Date	
Signature	

Please Mail to: Book Jungle
PO Box 2226
Champaign, IL 61825
or Fax to: 630-214-0564

ORDERING INFORMATION

web*: www.bookjungle.com*
email*: sales@bookjungle.com*
fax*: 630-214-0564*
mail*: Book Jungle PO Box 2226 Champaign, IL 61825*
or PayPal *to sales@bookjungle.com*

Please contact us for bulk discounts

DIRECT-ORDER TERMS

**20% Discount if You Order
Two or More Books**
Free Domestic Shipping!
Accepted: Master Card, Visa,
Discover, American Express

CPSIA information can be obtained
at www.ICGtesting.com
Printed in the USA
LVOW05s2341221216
518517LV00006B/88/P